Muffy, Fluffy, and D[exter]

in
Being Left Out Is Not Fun

Muffy   Dexter   Fluffy

By Lonia R. Broderick, Illustrator Al R. Broderick

Xulon PRESS

Muffy, Fluffy, and Dexter in BEING LEFT OUT IS NOT FUN
by Lonia R. Broderick, Illustrator Al R. Broderick

Printed in the United States of America

ISBN 9781626978485

www.xulonpress.com

Muffy, Fluffy, and Dexter

This one is for our two little miracles –
Eden and Delion, with love

"A man who has friends must himself be friendly, but there is a friend who sticks closer than a brother."
Proverbs 18:24 NKJV

HOW MANY MICE CAN YOU
FIND IN THIS BOOK?

IT WAS A new home and a new family, Fluffy was excited about that. She remembers when she first saw her new family come into the animal shelter. Then the most wonderful thing happened, they picked her and her sister, Muffy!

OVER IN A cage next to hers was another kitten, he was a boy. He was crying so loudly that her new owners decided to take him home too! His name was Dexter.

HER NEW OWNERS had two children, a boy and girl. They just loved their new kittens and always played with them when they got home from school.

THEIR NEW HOME was lovely too and there was a special place made just for them. It was filled with toys, places to sleep, and of course their food.

FLUFFY WAS USED to just playing with her sister, but now Muffy had a new friend, Dexter. She played with him often and Fluffy felt left out.

SHE WONDERED WHY Dexter did not play with her too. Day after day Fluffy would watch the two roll on the couch together, play tag, chase toys, and even nap together!

FLUFFY USUALLY JUST napped alone or sat around waiting for the children to come home and play with her.

SHE WOULD ALSO pass the time watching the birds from the window. She really enjoyed that, especially when they would sing.

ONE MORNING SHE watched her sister and Dexter chasing a small ball and hitting it back and forth to each other.

THEN ALL OF a sudden Dexter called out to Fluffy and asked if she wanted to play too. She wasted no time and jumped right into the game.

LATER THAT DAY Dexter went over to Fluffy and said, "Hey, that was a great game; I didn't know you could play so well!" "You never asked," said Fluffy. "Yeah, I know, but I didn't think you liked me," Dexter replied. "Why?" said Fluffy. "Well, you weren't friendly to me like your sister Muffy; I just thought you were mad that they adopted me, too," Dexter said, while looking down at the floor. "Oh no," said Fluffy, "I've always liked you; I'm just a little shy. I'm sorry I wasn't friendlier."

AFTER THAT FLUFFY was always a part of the fun and her lonely days a thing of the past. She had learned a very valuable lesson: to have friends, she must show herself friendly!

HOW MANY MICE DID YOU FIND?

CPSIA information can be obtained at www.ICGtesting.com
Printed in the USA
BVOW10s2234040813

327781BV00002B/2/P

9 781626 978485

Muffy, Fluffy, and Dexter in

Being Left Out Is Not Fun

Fluffy feels left out. Will she learn how to make new friends?

This book is the first from the Muffy, Fluffy, and Dexter series. Each book focuses on a specific scripture that applies to the lesson in the story. These faith-based books help aid parents and educators in teaching children about Godly character traits and how to apply them to their lives.

Lonia R. Broderick lives in North Carolina with her husband, Illustrator **Al R. Broderick,** their two children and their three cats. To learn more about the author and other books in this series, visit www.thewordsworking.com.

ISBN 978-1-62697-848-5

90000

xulon PRESS

9 781626 978485

A Bright House

by
Alix Schwartz
& Matt Geiler

illustrated by
MATT GEILER